Weekly Reader Children's Book Club presents

Marie Louise's Heyday

by Natalie Savage Carlson

pictures by Jose Aruego and Ariane Dewey

CHARLES SCRIBNER'S SONS
NEW YORK

*For Rosalys Hall, because
she is such a loyal friend*
N.S.C.

Text copyright © 1975 Natalie Savage Carlson
Illustrations copyright © 1975 Jose Aruego and Ariane Dewey

This book published simultaneously in the
United States of America and in Canada —
Copyright under the Berne Convention

All rights reserved. No part of this book
may be reproduced in any form without the
permission of Charles Scribner's Sons.

Printed in the United States of America
Library of Congress Catalog Card Number 75-8345
ISBN 0-684-14360-7

Weekly Reader Children's Book Club Edition

"Today is my heyday!" said Marie Louise.

Marie Louise was a little brown mongoose.
She lived with her mama in a thatched hut in a field
of sugarcane.

"Today is my heyday," she said, "because I have
found the sweetest, fattest banana on the Man's tree.
Now what shall I do when I get home? Shall I play
with my seashells and eat banana or swing in my swing
and eat banana or just eat banana?"

When she reached home, her mama decided for her.

"The possum mama just came by," she said. "She wants you to baby-sit with her children right away. She has to go to their grandpapa. He is having his fainting spells again."

Marie Louise sighed. "And on my heyday! How many children are there?"

"Five," said her mama.

"*Five!*" said Marie Louise. "I have to take care of *five* children?"

"The possum mama says they are very good children," said her mama. "They will probably sleep all day long."

Marie Louise set her banana down. She gave it a longing look.

Then off she hurried down the path through the sugarcane to the possums' tree house in the gumbo-limbo tree.

She climbed the thirty-three steps to the door.
She heard a big hubbub inside.

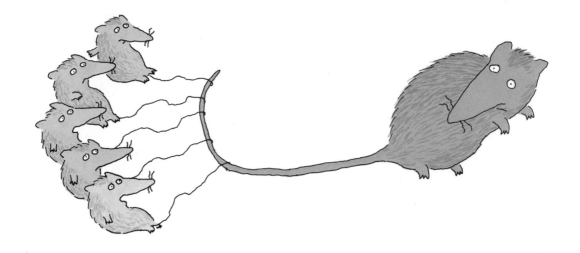

The five little possums were squealing and
squalling. They were clinging to their mama's tail
with all their might.

"Don't go away," begged one.

"Take us," begged another.

"We want to go, too," squealed a third.

"Stay," cried a fourth.

"Squeeeeeek," squeaked the fifth, louder than anybody.

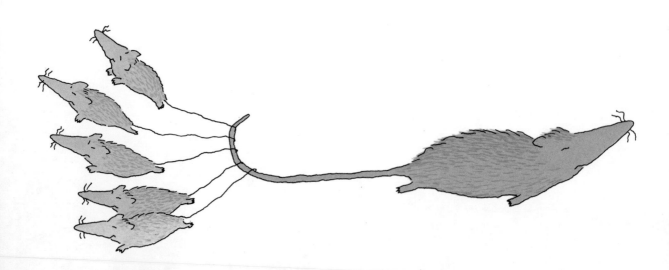

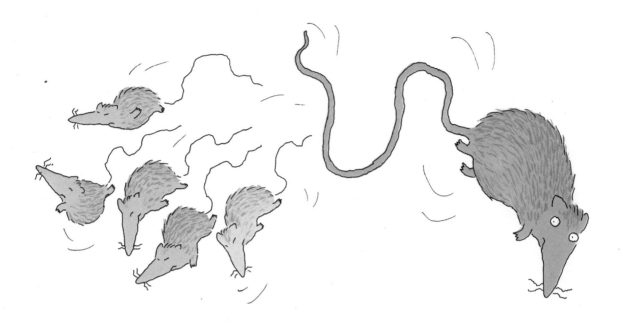

With a lurch the possum mama broke loose and hurtled toward the door. "They are very good children," she said to Marie Louise, as she hurried away.

The little possums stopped squealing and squalling. They gathered around Marie Louise. "What are your names?" she asked.

"I'm Jake,"
said one.

"I'm John,"
said another.

"I'm Lucie,"
said the third.

"I'm Lily,"
said the fourth.

"I'm Me,"
said the fifth.

"And I'm Marie Louise," said Marie Louise. "Now
let's go out and play."

"Shall we play tag?" asked Marie Louise.

"No," said Jake. "Let's play piggyback
like we do with mama."

He jumped on Marie Louise's back. He dug his
sharp little claws into her brown fur. They all jumped
on Marie Louise's back.
"Now take us for a ride," said Jake.

Marie Louise slowly crawled around the gumbo-limbo tree.

"Faster, faster," cried all the little possums.

Marie Louise tried to go faster but the load was too
heavy. Ten times she rode them around the gumbo-limbo tree.

"That's enough, children," she said. "Let's play
something else. How about patty-cake?"

"No. Let's play slide," said Jake.

He grabbed Marie Louise's long bushy tail. John grabbed Jake's tail. Lucie grabbed John's tail. Lily grabbed Lucie's tail. Me grabbed Lily's tail.

"Now take us for a slide," said Jake.

Marie Louise slowly pulled the string of little possums around the gumbo-limbo tree.

"Faster, faster," cried the five little possums.

But Marie Louise couldn't go any faster. The load was too heavy. She pulled them around the gumbo-limbo tree thirteen times.

"That will do," she panted. "It must be time for lunch. Let's go in the house." Marie Louise could hardly climb the thirty-three steps.

She went to the stove and peered into the big pot.
"Boiled greens," she said. "Your mama made some
good boiled greens for you."
She spooned the greens onto five little plates and
set one in front of each possum.

"I don't like boiled greens," said Jake.

"You should eat them anyway," said Marie Louise.
"They are full of vitamins. They will make your eyes
bright and your fur thick."

"I'm not hungry," said John.
"Isn't there something else?" asked Lucie.
"I want some scrambled eggs," said Lily.
Me said nothing. He only played in the greens with
his paws.

Marie Louise scraped the greens back into the pot.
"And to think that today started out to be my heyday!"
she sighed.

"Let's play some more," said Jake.

"You may go out and play while I'm washing the dishes,"
said Marie Louise. "But don't quarrel and don't go near
the stream and don't play roughly."

"We won't," cried all the little possums together.

"Children are very trying," said Marie Louise to the
pot on the stove. "It is so quiet and peaceful here without
them. It could almost be my heyday."

The dishes were nearly done when Lucie burst
through the door.
"Come quick!" she wailed. "Everybody's sick. I
feel sick, too. I think we're dying."

Marie Louise rushed down the thirty-three steps.
The little possums were moaning and groaning and
rolling on the ground.

"What's the matter?" cried Marie Louise.
Lucie pointed to a bush with shiny red berries.

"We ate those berries," she said. "My stomach aches."

"I'm burning inside," moaned Jake.

"My mouth is on fire," moaned Lily.

"I'm dying," moaned John.

"Me, too," moaned Me.

"*Poison berries!*" cried Marie Louise. "I'll run for the Witch Toad."

Marie Louise ran so fast that her tail could hardly
keep up with her. Then she had a frightening
thought. Perhaps the Witch Toad wasn't at home.
Maybe he had taken his magic brew to
Grandpapa Possum for his fainting spells.
She climbed the hill to the Witch Toad's house under
a big black rock. "Witch Toad! Witch Toad," she called.

"What's wrong with you?" asked the Witch Toad. "I've just come from visiting that old possum with his fainting spells."

"It's not me," gasped Marie Louise. "It's the possum children. They've eaten poison berries. I think they're dying."

"I'll bring my magic brew right away," said the Witch Toad, and they were on their way.

When they got back to the gumbo-limbo tree, Marie Louise held noses as the Witch Toad poured some of the magic brew down each little possum's throat.

"Ugh," said Jake.

"Bad," said John.

"No good," said Lucie.

"Phew," said Lily.

"Gulp," said Me.

Suddenly the little possums stopped moaning. They sat up and grinned.

"I feel bettter," said Jake.

"Cured," said John.

"Much better," said Lucie.

"I think I'll live," said Lily.

"Me, too," said Me.

"Where is my pay?" asked the Witch Toad.

Marie Louise didn't know how to pay him. Then she
climbed the thirty-three steps and fetched the pot of
boiled greens.

"I don't have any money," she said. "Will you take these boiled greens instead?"

The Witch Toad snatched the pot and looked at the greens.

"Looks like somebody's been playing in them with dirty paws," he grumbled.

"But I'll take them. They're full of vitamins," he said, and left.

The possum children gathered around Marie Louise.
"Why did you eat those berries?" she asked.

"Because I wanted to see
what they tasted like,"
said Jake.

"Because I wanted to,"
said Lucie.

"Because they
were so pretty,"
said John.

"Because the others did,"
said Lily.

"Just because,"
said Me.

"I'm hungry now," said Jake.

"I'm starved!" said Lucie.

"I want some boiled greens," said John.

"More magic brew," said Lily.

"Me, too," said Me.

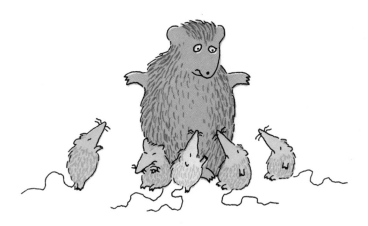

"You know there aren't any more boiled greens," said Marie Louise. "I had to give them to the Witch Toad. And he has taken his magic brew with him."

Just then the possum mama came walking up the steps.
"How did my children behave?" she asked Marie Louise.

"We were good,"
said Jake.

"Didn't quarrel,"
said Lucie.

"Didn't go near the stream,"
said John.

"Didn't play roughly,"
said Lily.

"Just ate some berries,"
said Me.

"I'm glad I'm me and not you," said Marie Louise to the possum mama and she left.

Marie Louise dragged herself home and she told her mama everything that had happened.

"But remember the time you wouldn't eat your mealy mush?" asked her mama. "Then you went out and chewed on a poison vine."

"I don't know why I did that," said Marie Louise. "Because I wanted to know what it tasted like, I guess. Or because it was so pretty. Or because I wanted to. Maybe, just because."

"Anyway you have your nice banana to eat now," said her mama.

"I'm too tired to eat anything," said Marie Louise. "I'll save it for my breakfast." And she climbed into her bed, and slept a long, long time.

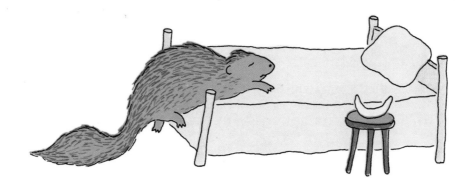

Next morning Marie Louise was awakened by a lot of chattering and giggling at the front door.

"Get up!" her mama called. "You have visitors."

Marie Louise jumped out of bed. She found the five little possums at the door.

"We've brought you
some flowers,"
said Jake.

"Because you saved
our lives,"
said Lucie.

"Because we love you,"
said John.

"Because we had so
much fun with you,"
said Lily.

"Just because,"
said Me.

"Will you baby-sit with us again?" they asked.

"Thank you," said Marie Louise, and she gathered the flowers
from their tails. "Yes, I'll baby-sit with you again sometime.
But not today," she added.

The little possums squealed with delight and scampered away.

"Children can be very trying sometimes,"
said Marie Louise to her mama.
She put the flowers in a vase and placed it
beside her plate on the breakfast table.
"But nobody ever gave me flowers before.
Today is really my heyday!"